Christmas 1997

To Christina:
With warm friendly thoughts.

Fondly,
Cynthia Holt Cummings

Christmas Friends

Christmas Friends

Teddy bear story in verse by
Cynthia Holt Cummings
Illustrated by
Fritz Henning

Holt Peterson Press

Birmingham, Michigan

Holt Peterson Press, Inc., Box 940
Birmingham, Michigan 48012

Printed in the United States of America
First printing, June 1996

ISBN 1-881811-11-5

Author's note

While the characters and locale of this story are fictitious and any perceived similarity to actual persons or places is specifically disclaimed, I acknowledge that the theme was inspired by an event which occurred early last October in Woodstock, Vermont at the peak of the "color season" while my husband and I were enjoying afternoon tea during our stay at The Woodstock Inn & Resort.

I am particularly grateful to Fritz Henning whose illustrations brought this story alive.

To Dick, my husband of 49 years, I give heartfelt thanks for his active support to a writing and publishing career which began at age 60. And to him I dedicate this book with love.

Surprise sat on a bench
On the Village Green,
The leaves were as bright
As he'd ever seen.

Red and gold
In their Autumn hue,
Over it all
A sky of blue.

A perfect spot
To discover the town,
As the buses and cars
Kept going around,

Bringing people
From far and near,
To enjoy the foliage
Every year.

Children played
In the Autumn leaves,
Jumping in piles
Way up to their knees.

Gathering leaves
Of red and gold,
For each of their hands
To gently hold.

Seasons would come
Seasons would go,
Soon all would be covered
With a blanket of snow.

Gold ribbon bows
Trimmed every wreath,
As bright as the gold
In the Autumn leaf.

Fur muffs and mittens
Warmed the cold air,
Christmas spirit
Was everywhere.

Sleigh bells would ring
Laughter would sound,
As the sleighs passed the Green
In this country town.

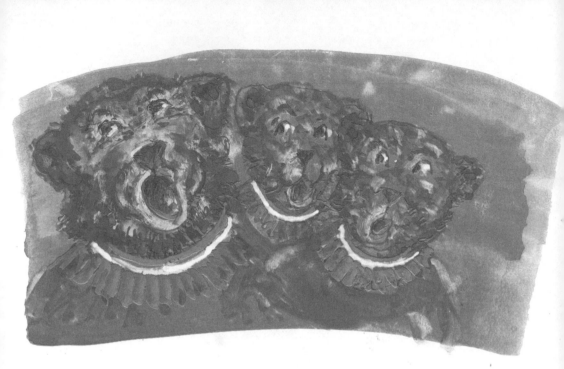

How many years
He'd heard sleigh bells ring,
How many years
He'd heard voices sing:

"Joy to the World"
And "Silent Night,"
"Away in a Manger"
When the Star was bright.

Strange how friends meet
But it happened this day,
On the Village Green
In the strangest way.

"JJ" a mouse
In this country town,
Planned to live at the Inn
The whole year round.

21

But somehow at tea
She got in the way,
Was put out of the Inn
With no place to stay.

She scampered across
To the Village Green,
Hid under the leaves
Where she couldn't be seen.

Surprise looked down
And suddenly saw,
Some movement that began
To tickle his paw.

He was as startled
As any bear,
To see a tiny mouse
Jump up in the air.

"JJ" looked at Surprise
And hoped she had found,
A friendly bear
In this country town.

She told him her plight
With no place to stay,
And they became friends
In the strangest way.

Surprise discovered
On the Green this day,
How friendship was a gift
To be given away.

He took "JJ" home
To the family of bears,
Who lived in the house
With circular stairs.

"JJ" was small
And hard to see,
But they welcomed her in
To the Bear family.

Mandy placed a pillow
In one of the chairs,
And "JJ" became part
Of the family of bears.

She sat on the pillow
Proud as could be,
This little mouse
With personality.

Her manners were perfect
In every way,
She listened carefully
To what each would say.

She learned how to climb
Up the circular stairs,
And became so happy
With the family of bears.

The news soon spread
All around,
How a bear and a mouse
Became friends in this town.

People would stare
As they went down the street,
But they gave a big smile
To all they would meet.

After a while
The stares went away,
As the town saw their friendship
Was here to stay.

One day Surprise taught her
To make mittens of red,
While they talked about cheese
And honey on bread.

They made up a song
They all could sing,
And thought of the happiness
Their voices would bring,

To all of the shut-ins
In that country town,
On Christmas Eve
With the snow coming down.

The family of bears
Learned one day,
How the church needed gifts
To be given away.

Surprise and JJ
Went into town,
Visited shops
And quickly found,

Candy and toys
They could give away,
To the families in need
On Christmas Day.

Surprise and "JJ"
Filled paper sacks,
With candy canes
And jumping jacks.

Toy trumpets of brass
And lollipops,
Ribbon candy
And chocolate drops.

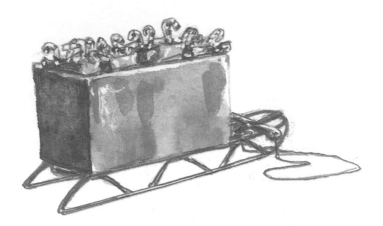

They went to the church
Across the way,
To donate these gifts
To be given away.

The family of bears
Decided one day,
A big surprise
For their friend "JJ".

53

They would go together
Promptly at three,
To be at the Inn
For the Christmas tea.

They wrapped a gift
In gold and green,
With white ribbon bows
That could be easily seen.

A gift of friendship
"JJ" would bring,
To share with all
Having tea at the Inn.

The family of Bears was as proud
As could be,
When they arrived with "JJ"
For the Christmas tea.

The staff was surprised
When they came through the door,
Could this be the mouse
They had seen months before?

She took off her coat
Her fur muff and hat,
Went to a table
And gently sat,

In a chair with a pillow
As high as could be,
Then Surprise brought her cookies
With a cup of tea.

The pretty wrapped gift
Was by her chair,
She looked around
To see who was there.

They were laughing and talking
Drinking their tea,
Just like "JJ"
And the Bear Family.

The piano was playing
A Christmas song,
"JJ" listened
And before very long,

She saw a guest sitting
By herself in a chair,
And thought of the friendship
She wanted to share.

There in the corner
Was a tree all aglow,
Where presents were placed
In piles below.

Wrapped in pretty paper
For all to see,
"JJ" put her gift
Under the tree.

When her gift was opened
After the tea,
They found a bright star
From the Bear Family,.

With a message inside
Written in gold:
"This is "JJ's" friendship
For your hearts to hold."

As people stood
On the Village Green,
Rays of light
Could be easily seen,

From the star in a window
Of the Inn that night,
Bringing friendship to all
With its Christmas light.

The town would never
Be quite the same,
As prayers were said
In His sacred name.

Surprise and "JJ"
Went on their way,
Friends forever
From this Christmas Day.

Merry Christmas to all
With blessings too,
Just "being a friend"
Is their gift to you.

The Author

Cynthia Holt Cummings, born in West Boylston, Massachusetts, graduated from Massachusetts General Hospital School for Nurses. During WWII, she served in the Army Nurse Corps with that hospital's reactivated unit. . . . 6th General. . . . from May 1942 to February 1946 including 33 months in North Africa and Italy.

Since 1948 she has lived in the Birmingham, Michigan area as a homemaker with her husband, Dick, now retired. Their son, Roger, named after her youngest brother an Air Force gunner killed during WWII, is married to Buff and lives nearby with their four children. . . . David, Julie, Jessica and Amanda.

In 1979 Cynthia's Christmas poetry written over the years for family and friends was consolidated and printed as that year's holiday greeting card. Accepting her husband's challenge, nine other books of new Christmas poetry, including four teddy bear stories, have since been published.

The Artist

The son of a noted illustrator, Fritz Henning grew up in the environs of an art studio and upon graduation from New York Maritime College, served as a ship's officer for a number of years before becoming a professional artist.

Long associated with the North Light Publications and with the Famous Artists School, Henning has been constantly involved in the world of visual art, including illustration, painting, designing, teaching and writing about the way of art and artists.

Recently retired to New Hampton, New Hampshire, Henning and his wife Jane have four children and 13 grandchildren.

Other illustrated books of Christmas poetry and verse by Cynthia Holt Cummings initially published in the indicated year by Holt Peterson Press, Inc., Box 940, Birmingham, Michigan 48012.

Teddy bear stories in verse:

Christmas Bells, 1995
Christmas Spirit, 1989
Christmas Joy, 1986
Christmas Surprise, 1985

Collections of short poems:

Christmas Treasures, 1988
Christmas Wishes, 1987
Christmas Love, 1984
Christmas Memories, 1982
Christmas Ribbons, 1980

Deluxe edition of previously published short Christmas poems with full color illustration by Fritz Henning:

Christmas Dreams, 1992

Author narration on audio cassettes also available.